It's Always a Good Day for Crabbing

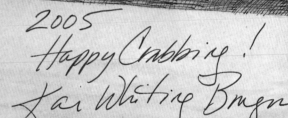

2005
Happy Crabbing!
Kai Whiting Burgess

By Karin Whiting Burgess
Illustrated by Deborah McLaren

FLAT HAMMOCK PRESS

MYSTIC, CONNECTICUT

Flat Hammock Press
5 Church Street
Mystic, Connecticut 06355
860.572.2722
www.flathammockpress.com

ISBN: 0-9718303-4-7

Printed in the United States of America

First printing

10 9 8 7 6 5 4 3 2 1

For more information on illustrator Deborah McLaren
please visit www.deborahmclaren.com

In the summer, gray or blue
We go crabbing, me and Lu.

Found my bucket and my line.
Grab a hot dog. Mom said fine.

Got a hook and a rock.
I could do this round-the-clock!

On the dock, Lu takes a look.
I poke the hot dog with my hook.

Drop it in, down it goes.

Lu sniffs sea air with her nose.

Peeking over. Nothing yet.
Soon I'll get one, I just bet!

Seaweed sways and hides my bait
Yes, I got one. Count to eight.

Carefully, I pull him near,
My pail is set for the crab's premiere.

Hold on my friend, we're almost there,
Fall in my bucket, not mid-air!

Finally safe down in the water
That crab scratches round, a real hot rodder.

My crab is so hungry,
I plunk in a treat.
A piece of hot dog that was at my feet.

Back to my line. Down it goes.
So busy now, no time to doze.

Here they come, I drop them in,
Crawling and snapping, chaos on tin.

Large and small crabs edged in blue
I've surely got more than yesterday's few.

Go away Mr. Sea Gull, don't snag my bait!
I'll give you some later. You just have to wait.

A man on the dock admires my catch.
Together we watch them, a furious batch!

Back to the sea. Time now to go.
Tip over the bucket and watch them...

...WHOAAA!

Across the dock they scuttle and drop.
Off the edge they fall with a big belly flop.

Now they're happy, back in their home.
Again among seaweed and rocks they will roam.

Here Mr. Sea Gull, have a good snack.
I'll see you tomorrow.

I WILL be back!